W9-CAI-308

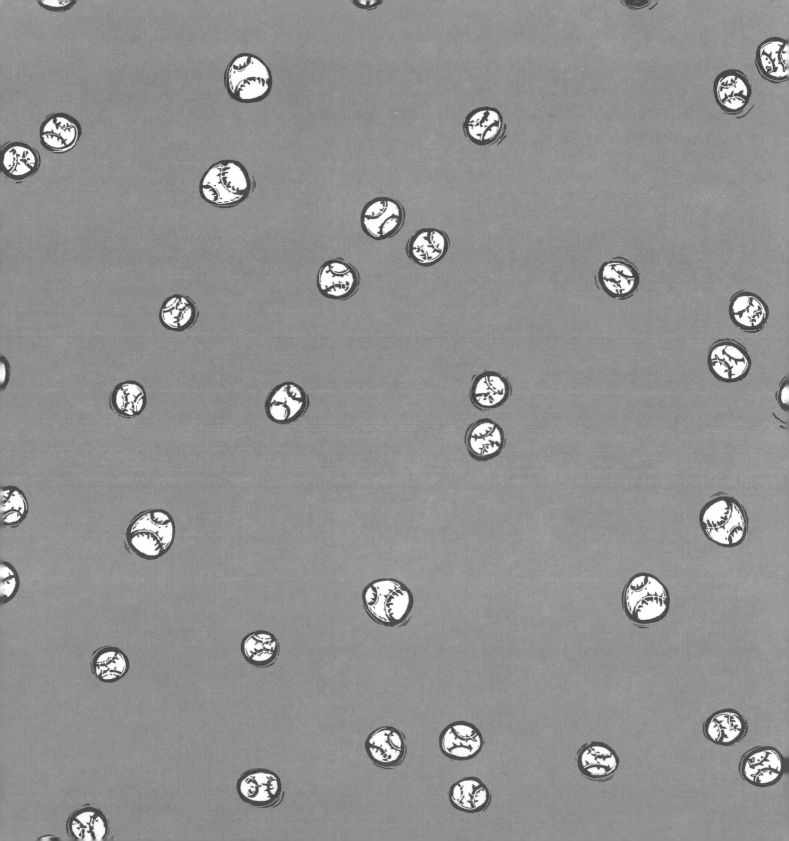

BATS ABOUT BASEBALL

By Jean Little & Claire Mackay
Illustrated by Kim LaFave

VIKING

Ryder's grandmother was bats about baseball.
On his first birthday, she gave him baseball pajamas.
When he turned two, she got a Blue Jays pennant
for his room.
When he turned three, she gave him a baseball cap
and nine baseball cards from her own collection.
When he turned four, she gave him a bat and a ball.
When he turned five, she gave him a catcher's mitt.
And as soon as he learned to read, she bought him
a baseball dictionary.
She was crazy.

Even when she was babysitting him, Ryder's
Nana went right on being bats about baseball.
Once the baseball season started, it wasn't easy
to talk with her about anything else.
But Ryder kept trying.

"Nana," he said, "do you think I should be
an ornithologist when I grow up? I could be like
Grandpa Winger and study birds."

Nana flew to the TV and turned it on.

"The Jays play the Orioles today," she said.
She nestled down into the big chair. Ryder
perched beside her.

"Nana, listen to me," Ryder said. "I could run
a chicken farm like Aunt Henriette when I grow up."

"Lay off, you turkey! What do you mean 'foul'?"
Nana shouted at the umpire. "What a dumb cluck!"

What a birdbrain! Ryder thought, grinning.

"Pay attention to ME!" he said. "I could be a mathematician when I grow up."

"Three and two, full count. This guy's 0 for 19. Strike three!" yelled Nana. "Three up, three down!"

Ryder left the room. He came back with his baseball cap on his head, his catcher's mitt on his hand and his bat on his shoulder.
He marched back and forth in front of the TV.
Then Nana paid attention.

"Ryder, move!" she said. "You make a better door than a window."

Ryder moved to the window. He stared at the sky.

"Nana," he said, "when I grow up, maybe I could be an astronaut like Cousin Stella."

"By Jupiter!" Nana said, "Casey just launched a moon shot right into the Sky Deck."

Ryder didn't speak to her for two whole innings.
He didn't watch the game either. He read his book.
Nana didn't even notice.

Then Ryder leapt from the back of his chair to the couch to the coffee table. The TV guide, the baseball dictionary and Ryder hit the floor together.

"I've made up my mind," he announced. "I'm going to be a ballet dancer like my Mum when I grow up."

"Okay, Blue Jays, on your toes," Nana said. "This guy's famous for dying swans."

Ryder giggled. His mother had danced in *Swan Lake* last winter.

Ryder climbed on the couch and growled.
He glared at Nana.

"Or maybe I'll be an animal trainer like Uncle Lionel when I grow up," he said.

"This pitcher's wild," Nana roared. "Why don't they get Felix out of the bullpen? He used to be a Tiger."

They did go to the bullpen. While the new pitcher trotted across the field, Nana got out her junk food. With the first pitch, Ryder pilfered some peanuts and swiped a fistful of caramel corn.

"Maybe I ought to be a kleptomaniac." He waited. What would she say to that?

Nana didn't bat an eye.

"It's a dazzling double steal!" she said. "What a crackerjack play!"

Nana must be making jokes on purpose.
Ryder decided to throw her a curve.

"Nana, I think I might like to be a deep sea diver
like your friend Marlin."

Nana had a comeback ready.
"What a great sinker!" she said.

Ryder choked. Then he tried turning a cartwheel. He fell over with a crash. Nana never took her eyes off the screen.

"Or I could be a chiropractor like Uncle Bonaparte when I grow up," Ryder said.

Nana stretched. "Now we need some back-to-back hits to break out of our slump."

Bats about baseball! That's what she was. Bats. That gave Ryder a new idea.

"Maybe I'll be a spelunker when I grow up," he said.

"Don't cave in now, with the heavy bats up next," said Nana.

Ryder stared at her. How long could she keep this up?

"Stay low and inside or he'll go deep on you," his grandmother told the pitcher.

She could keep it up forever.

Suddenly the lights flickered. Then the room went pitch black.

"The power's off, Nana." Ryder's voice was gleeful. "It's game over."

"It's just a time out, kid," said his grandmother. She got something out of her bag. "I've got all the bases covered."

He could hear the smile in her voice as she switched on her radio.

The lights and the TV came on again.

Ryder went back to the game he and Nana were playing with words.

"Maybe I'll be an airline pilot like my Dad when I grow up," he said.

Nana propelled herself into the air.

"It's a pop fly!" she bellowed. "He's out!"

Ryder collapsed onto the couch laughing.
Nana collapsed into her chair moaning.

"Oh, my poor old bones," she gasped. "I should know better at my age."

Ryder got up and started out of the room.
At the door, he paused.

"Maybe I'll be a paleontologist," he said, "and search for evidence of ancient life. I could start with you."

He heard her laughing as he ran down the hall.

"What flavour, Nana?" he yelled.

"Banana," said Nana.

He got two popsicles from the freezer, a lime for him and a banana for her.
When he came back, a commercial was on the TV.
A sailboat skimmed across the screen. Ryder tried a new tack.

"Maybe I won't even wait to grow up. I'll run away and join the navy!"

"Two aboard, and a big gun on deck," Nana said. "He was traded from the Pirates. We're sunk."

"One more like that, Nana, and you'll walk… the plank," said Ryder.

Ryder slurped up the last of his popsicle and said in a loud voice, "I might be a guitarist in a rock band when I grow up."

Nana cheered.

"Perfect pitch!" she said.
"Now he's really into his rhythm."

It was the bottom of the ninth. The score was tied.
Nana was on her feet, pacing.

"Get a hit, get a hit, GET A HIT!" she chanted.
"Whack it, smack it!"

"Smack it, whack it!" yelled Ryder, getting into the
swing of the thing. "Hey, Nana, when I grow up,
I could be a famous poet."

"It's a homer!" Nana shrieked. "What an epic game!"

The Jays were jumping for joy. Nana beamed at Ryder.

"Did you want something, dear?" she asked.

Ryder smiled at her.

"Nana," he said softly, "what are *you* going to be when you grow up?"

This book is for Tom Cheek and Jerry Howarth, who let blind people like me see every game. — J.L.

To Ryder Gordon Mohler Mackay, my world champion grandson. — C.M.

For Cameron and Jeffrey. — K.L.

VIKING
Published by the Penguin Group
Penguin Books Canada Ltd, 10 Alcorn Avenue, Toronto, Ontario, Canada M4V 3B2
Penguin Books Ltd, 27 Wrights Lane, London W8 5TZ, England
Viking Penguin, a division of Penguin Books USA Inc., 375 Hudson Street,
New York, New York 10014, U.S.A.
Penguin Books Australia Ltd, Ringwood, Victoria, Australia
Penguin Books (NZ) Ltd, 182-190 Wairau Road, Auckland 10, New Zealand

Penguin Books Ltd, Registered Offices: Harmondsworth, Middlesex, England

First published 1995

1 3 5 7 9 10 8 6 4 2

Text copyright © Jean Little and Claire Mackay, 1995
Illustrations copyright © Kim LaFave, 1995

*Publisher's note: This book is a work of fiction. Names, characters, places and incidents
either are the product of the author's imagination or are used fictitiously, and any
resemblance to actual persons living or dead, events, or locales is entirely coincidental.*

Printed and bound in Hong Kong on acid neutral paper

Canadian Cataloguing in Publication Data

Little, Jean, 1932-
Bats about baseball

ISBN 0-670-85270-8

I. Title.

PS8523.I8733 1995   jC813'.54   C94-931640-7
PZ7.L57Ba 1995

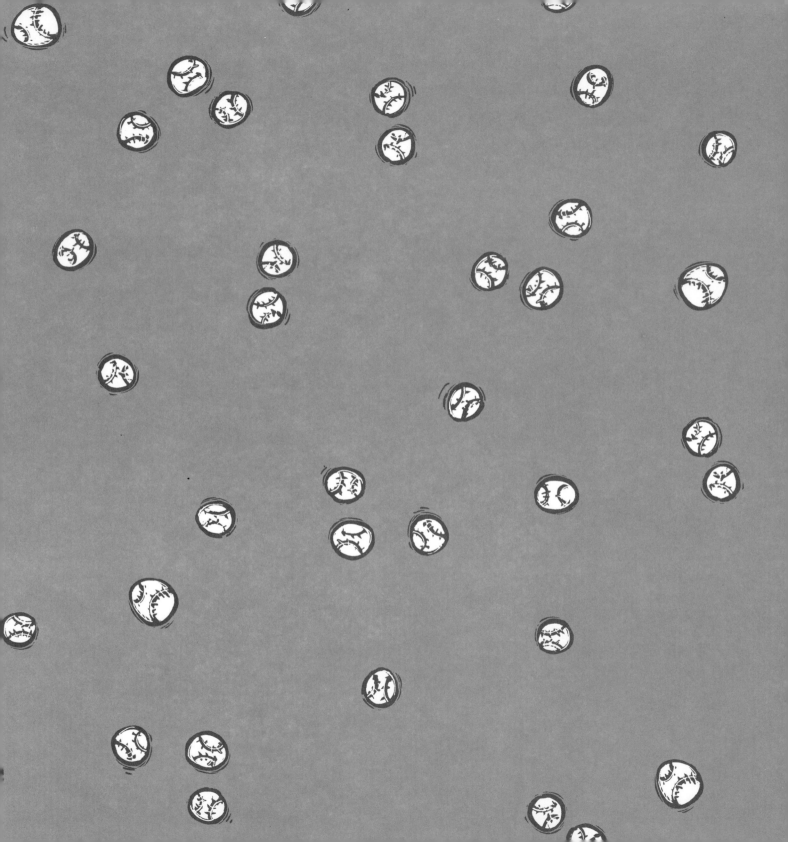